Little Me

My First Day of School

STEPHANIE HUGHES

AuthorHouse™ UK
1663 Liberty Drive
Bloomington, IN 47403 USA
www.authorhouse.co.uk
UK TFN: 0800 0148641 (Toll Free inside the UK)
UK Local: 02036 956322 (+44 20 3695 6322 from outside the UK)

Because of the dynamic nature of the Internet, any web addresses or links contained in
this book may have changed since publication and may no longer be valid. The views
expressed in this work are solely those of the author and do not necessarily reflect the views
of the publisher, and the publisher hereby disclaims any responsibility for them.

Any people depicted in stock imagery provided by Getty Images are models,
and such images are being used for illustrative purposes only.
Certain stock imagery © Getty Images.

This book is printed on acid-free paper.

ISBN: 978-1-6655-9232-1 (sc)
ISBN: 978-1-6655-9233-8 (e)

Print information available on the last page.

Published by AuthorHouse 09/24/2021

authorHOUSE®

Introduction

Stephanie Hughes, the author of this children's story is diagnosed with autism. Autistic Spectrum Disorder (ASD). This children's storybook tells a story of Isla, a girl with autistic spectrum disorder, and her experiences on her first day of school. She is frightened by crowds, new people and noises. Isla has communication difficulties, but she makes it to the end of the day and now she knows what it is like, it makes her better prepared to go back tomorrow.

ASD is a lifelong developmental disability. It affects how people communicate and it can cause extreme anxiety. Autistic people much prefer to have routines, and really dislike change. Some people with the disorder may only eat certain foods, wear the same type of clothes every day, travel the same way to certain places. Changes in their routine can cause great distress, making them more anxious, for example changing school, or starting school for the first time. Christmas is a big change, holidays or food cooked a different way.

Sensitivities; taste, touch, sound and lights. Lights may be too bright, sounds can be loud to some, like a TV, a bus or crowds. Food has so many flavours and textures that it's just too much for some people. This is why it's important for them to develop coping mechanisms like wearing headphones if it's too loud, using fidget toys if they are feeling anxious.

Every autistic person is different, and have different needs. Other traits of ASD could be taking things very literal, not understanding jokes, being very sensitive, finding it hard to form and keep friendships, they may have special interests and become highly focused on them. It is all very intense and can lead to autistic burnout and meltdowns.

I hope this book helps you to relate to Islas first day at school in the eyes of an autistic child.

To my four beautiful children — Josh, Macey, Florence and Nancy; My world.

My first day of school
starts early today.
I wish I understood and
knew how to play.

So many questions – where do I start?
How will I learn? I only love art.

We are nearly there; I can
see all the crowds.
My stomach feels sick;
it's spinning around.

I have to leave Mum; when
we get to the gate.
When will I see her? It's
a long time to wait.

My clothes are so itchy;
I'm not even comfy.
We all wear the same; I
guess that is something.

I like things the same – all
my food and my stuff.
I wish they understood me;
I wish I was enough.

The classroom is big; there
are tables everywhere.
All the other children,
don't seem to care.

It's so loud for me here; I wish
I could hide under a table.
But then they would laugh
and see I'm unable —

Unable to talk, even ask for some help.
I need to go to the toilet, but
I won't go by myself.

I'm afraid of the children, the
noise and the smells.
The voice of the teacher, is
like ringing some bells.

Isla's my name; I told a
boy when he asked.

But I'm not good at talking,
So off he went on past.

Lunchtime arrives; it's
so loud and scary.
This room is so huge that
it makes me wary.

Food is a worry; I'm frightened to eat.
The smell and the colour –
I'm scared what I'll meet.

At home I eat the same food every day.
I know what to expect, and
I like things that way.

I sit next to a girl; her name
is Mia McGraph.
She smiles at me and then
makes me laugh.

We finish our lunch; then
she asks me to play.
"Really? Me?" I thought.
This has made my day.

It makes me so happy;
I'm really so shy.
I'm scared of new people,
and things and may cry.

But I'm just a little girl looking for fun.
I want to be myself; I want to fit in.

I will wear my headphones if
it's loud and I'm scared.
Sometimes I'll sit, and I
won't say a word.
The world is so busy, and
it's all a big blur.

If you didn't know, then this is all me.
My name is Isla, and I have ASD.

ASD, is a part of me;
I feel different inside; it's
hard for people to see.

All of my life; they say I'm unique.
My brain is like a puzzle, and
I sometimes can't speak.

I look at the world in a different way.
I love animals, and I hate
Christmas Day.

The day's nearly done;
I'm so tired now.
I want to relax; but I don't know how.

I don't sleep at night; my
mind is so busy.
Even while I sit here, my
thoughts make me dizzy.

At home, I had tea and drove
Mum 'round the bend.
Now I'm in my bed; I made
it until the end.

Tomorrow I'll go back;
yes, I'll be scared.
Now I've been once, though,
my mind's more prepared.

All I can do is just be me –
A little girl called Isla who has ASD.

The end.

Please just remember: we
are not all the same.
Everyone is different; nobody
should be ashamed.

Just be patient, and give it some time.
You are so special, and I
hope you now realise.

Isla has autism, today is her first day
of school, how will she cope? Will she
manage to get through the day?

———————◆———————

A truly heartfelt story, that will open
your eyes and make you believe that
Uniqueness is greatness.

———————◆———————

It's ok to be different.

author HOUSE®

ISBN 978-1-6655-9232-1

51290

9 781665 592321

Grandad's Story

**Language, maths and science activities
based on a lively family story.**

How to use this book

This story/activity book has been specially written to help young children – and their parents – prepare for school. The story centres around Jenny, Baby and their family. Share the story with your child and talk about Jenny and Baby's family and the things that happen to them.

Begin by reading through the story together.

Try the activities after you've read the story – they can be tackled in any order.

Each activity appears on a different background colour, depending on the main focus of the activity:

> yellow denotes a language-based activity;
> blue denotes a maths-based activity;
> pink denotes a science-based activity.

Brief notes on what your child learns through doing these activities, and ideas for more things to do, can be found on page 32.

Many of the activities suggest simple things you can do at home using everyday household objects, or outside in your immediate environment. They encourage children to talk about the story and what they see in the pictures, to stretch their imaginations, and to talk about their own experiences. Children learn best by doing things; and talking helps them to make sense of what they have done.

Learning at home

We all learn best within a framework which is relaxed and secure, and we all need praise and encouragement. Keep this in mind as you're working through the activities with your child.

It's sometimes difficult to judge how much your child can and can't do at a particular age. Every child is different, and needs to develop at their own pace. Don't expect too much. If your child is having problems with an activity, be patient and explain it to them simply and clearly. (The notes on page 32 will help.) At times, it may be advisable to come back to an activity at a later stage when your child is more ready to tackle it.

Ready for school

One of the best ways to ensure that your child will settle down well at school is to help them become familiar with books, and to share lots of stories with them. There are many enjoyable activities which you can do with your child at home, which will help them when they start school. Encourage them to take an interest in everything around them, whether it be the shape of words on a page, the number of plates on a table, or why a ball always comes down when it is thrown up in the air. Develop that sense of curiosity, wonder and excitement at an early age, because it will be of immeasurable benefit as more formal work is introduced at school.